Dark Romance

Extremely Domination, Alpha, Monster Cuckold, Menage

Age Gap, Erotica Romance Story

Lana Kendra

it wasn't bought for your personal use only, go back to your favorite ebook retailer and buy your copy. Thank you for acknowledging this author's efforts.

Table of Contents

Content Warning

Due to its sexual content, this book is only for those over the age of legal adulthood. There are some topics with a lot of foul language. All of the characters are at least eighteen years old.

Introduction

Are you in search of an exciting and thrilling book to read? Look no further than this extensive collection of Erotic Suspense book. I offer a wide range of genres, including Romantic Erotica, Fantasy, and Urban BDSM Fiction, to cater to even the most discerning reader. Whether you enjoy Anthologies, Westerns, or Paranormal Romance, I have something to suit your taste. My collection also includes Poetic Folklore, Interracial, Black & African American Literary Criticism, and Gothic Horror for those who crave a deeper and darker reading experience. If you're interested in Futuristic, LGBTQ+, Short Stories, or Lesbian literature, my diverse range of options will keep you captivated. Additionally, I offer Humorous, Victorian, New Adult, and College Women's Psychological Mysteries for those seeking a lighter but equally engaging read. Furthermore, My Fairy Tale Collections,

Transgender, Contemporary Western, Bisexual, and Poetry genres will transport you to different worlds and explore a variety of themes. For my Teen and Young Adult readers, I have a selection of European Geography, Cultures, eBooks, Loners, Outcasts, Mythology, Folk Tales, and much more. With such a wide array of options to choose from, you'll never run out of thrilling and enchanting stories to immerse yourself in.

It is important to emphasize that this content is exclusively intended for individuals who are 18 years of age or older.

Dark Romance

"So Princess, I've got an interesting job for you for next Wednesday," James said. "You up for it?"

James appeared to be content with both the world and himself as he sat on the couch in his apartment. My extremely happy client had just departed, having paid a respectable amount for my services. I was returning from tidying up and putting on my street clothes again. I took a seat in the chair across from him.

As you might have surmised, James is my agency, and I like to think of myself as a part-time party girl. Though he has a few other redeeming features, he's not the most polished gem in the jeweler's window and has other terminology for our various jobs. I was first introduced to this business by James.

Just to give you a little overview, I met her when I was a

senior in college and I went to visit the Village with a few other girls. We were joined by James, who "showed us around". As a result, I took several actions that I otherwise would not have taken. Later, James offered to sell me the incriminating material, which he showed me. He suggested that I work it out by putting out for him and a few other guys who he said would pay generously for my services when I told him I couldn't raise the type of money he was requesting. Not that I had many options. It took several sessions to pay him back, and in that time, I was pleasantly surprised to find that I was talented at the task and that I actually kind of enjoyed it. Additionally, during the weeks of my indenture, even though James and I have very different backgrounds, we managed to acquire a grudging respect for one another. I therefore took him up on his offer of a more long-term arrangement when my "debt" was settled. I'm not a moron, though; I continued working as a copywriter for a city legal company during the day. Thus, the term "part-time."

Since we've been doing this for a while, we've established a solid working rapport and seen significant financial success. I paid attention when he told me he had a "interesting job" for me.

I didn't notice the tinge of irony in his voice, so I assume I was feeling quite good about the rather satisfying job I had just done on my client, and maybe even still wrapped in the delightful warmth of a couple of really good orgasms. However, I was aware from past encounters that James's notion of a 'interesting' task did not consistently align with my own.

"I'm not sure if I like the term 'interesting,'" I remarked with some uncertainty. "But I'm listening."

"Ok. The guy is a bit of a geek. He does something with computers on Wall Street. All I know is that it pays good.

He probably makes more in a day than you or I do in a month. So, the pay for this one is great. We're talkin' upwards of five hundred or more, if you do him good."

"Mmm. So far so good. Incall or outcall?"

"Out."

" James," I replied, "you know I don't like outcalls. Risky. I prefer working on our own turf and having you in the next room if anything goes pear-shaped."

"I know, Babe," he comfortingly uttered. "I met this guy in person and laid out the terms. And the circumstances are such that it has to be in his own apartment. He knows he's got to make it worthwhile. And he knows what'll happen to him if he damages you. Anyway, you've done a couple of outcalls before, and they've worked out fine, haven't they?"

"It's still my ass on the line, not yours."

"Quit worrying. That's my job. I ain't gonna risk you or your cute little ass. Worth too much to me."

How endearingly kind. My knightly defender. However, I was aware that he was being truthful. Moreover, he described my ass as "cute." It was quite nice.

He smiled and continued, "One more detail." "It's a costume gig."

"Oh shit," I exclaimed. "I'm not dressing up in some damn cheerleader outfit again. I looked ridiculous!"

Why do guys like dressing up? Why do they sometimes need to put up a front in order to get it on? What's wrong with a classic, down-home fuck?

"Not a cheerleader," James declared. "You're gonna be a professional. You oughta like that. And hey, you looked great in that cheerleader outfit."

"Mmm. Maybe. What kind of professional?"

"Guy wants a nurse. He likes to pretend he's sick and needs special treatment."

"Interesting. What kind of 'special treatment'? Did he say?"

"Nope. He left it up to you. So be creative."

I enjoy a good challenge.

It was a bitterly cold and overcast Wednesday. It was windier that night, but not much better. I made a quick stop at James's to change into the new nurse's uniform he got. He refused to reveal exactly where he had obtained it. But it fit every curve and was incredibly sexy— James finally got my measurements down correct. White high heels, virtually transparent white nylon bikini underwear, a tight white skirt with a split up the right side, sheer white nylons with lacy elastic bands on top, and a tight-fitting white shirt with minimal buttons over a lacy white bra with a hook in the front were all seen. It was one of those push-up bras with underwire. My natural cleavage has never been criticized, but what it did for me had to be against the law. I adored that!

I was relieved the weather was chilly so I could layer an overcoat over my clothes. I'd be too afraid to be seen in it on the streets for fear of getting arrested or sexually assaulted, or both.

I was worried as I got a cab to the address James had given me, even though he had reassured me. The fact that the cabbie almost caused an accident by staring into the rearview mirror rather than the street didn't help either. He left cheerfully, but with a very bad tip.

It was a midtown apartment building, quite costly. Doorman included. The elegant doorman was unimpressed when I told him why I was there. He simply made a call, received approval, and took me to the elevator. I suppose that prior to me, there were other "nurses." That wouldn't be too horrible, actually. I'm naturally competitive, and I have a good sense of my own strengths. I prefer a challenge, like I mentioned.

I gave the door a rap. While being examined via the spy hole, there was a pause, and then the door opened, so suddenly that I nearly fell back. It was a woman who opened the door!

I was going to kill James if he ruined my client's sex. It's not like I hadn't dated before, but it wasn't my first option, and he ought to have told me so I could have prepared a bit differently. If I'm saying something significant, sexy for a guy isn't always sexy for a woman.

"Please enter," she pleaded. She appeared appealing in a mousy sort of way, with a clear complexion and short, dark hair, as viewed through the doorway. Her complexion immediately made me wonder what I could do with it; she wasn't going to significantly increase Sephora's stock, though. She looked up at me once, and then only once during our conversation. If not, she devoted herself to one of the walls nearby or to my waist.

She said, "You have to be here for my husband." "That man, James, sent you?"

Finding my voice took a few moments. I had no idea what would come next.

"Yes," I accomplished. How could I put it?

"I gather from your expression that James didn't give you all the details," she responded. "Please understand that I love my husband, but he has rather idiosyncratic tastes in sex, and I am not willing or able to indulge him in many of them. That's where you come in. I don't mind; it keeps him happy and frees me. I look on it as just hiring another professional like a doctor or psychiatrist."

At least she gave useful examples. I guess she could have said "dog walker."

"I think I understand," I answered, grinning my most comforting smile at her. In my opinion, though, I could never hope to be as giving as she was in a situation like this. I was starting to feel conflicted, even furious at her, even though I was really trying to be empathetic. I was unable to understand her. Had she fallen victim to a deceptive deal in exchange for wealth and safety, and was now going to great lengths to hold onto them? Or was she merely attempting to maintain her sense of dignity because she truly loved her husband?

Anyway. Her intention was for me to have sex with her husband, not for me to condemn her. I have to act with professionalism.

"May I meet your husband?"

"Certainly. And thank you for understanding. Here, let me take your coat. I see that it's quite wet out there."

I gave her my coat. She gave me a really close inspection. I'm used to getting checked out before a meeting by now, but usually by men. This was somewhat unique. But apparently I passed inspection, for she grinned, although a little wistfully, I felt.

"May I say that you are a very beautiful woman," she responded. "You have a gorgeous body, and that costume fits you very well. You also seem to be quite intelligent and a cut above the others who have been here. Gregg is going to be most happy."

She guided me back inside the apartment, passing by a very tasteful modern living room with highlights of gold in the form of lamps and vases, and a predominantly black and white color scheme. Not really my taste. She gestured toward a hallway door.

"That's our bedroom, or for tonight, Gregg's 'sickroom'. Just knock and go right in. I'll be waiting here when you and he are done. Oh, and here's your fee. Is this correct?"

Yes, it was. Whoa, that was it!

Without saying anything further, she turned and returned to the living room. I was relieved she wasn't accompanying me inside. Even though she appeared aloof, I doubted it would be enjoyable for her to witness her spouse and I engaging in sexual activity. In addition, I felt more liberated to employ my skills however I saw fit.

I gave the door a rap.

Something said, "Come in," from inside.

When I walked in, I noticed a man in a very tastefully

furnished modern bedroom, lying behind a dark silk sheet on a king-sized bed. To me, it didn't really resemble a sickroom. The man, who I assumed to be Gregg, was lying on pillows. He was bare where the covering did not cover him. He appeared to be in his late thirties and had nice looks. He most definitely didn't appear ill. That should come as no surprise.

He gave me a very close inspection. It was obvious he enjoyed what he saw.

Opposite the bed was a chair facing the 'patient'. Making sure the cut in my skirt opened to reveal my legs up to the lacy tops of my stockings, I sat down and crossed my legs. My well-proportioned, long legs can be used to subtly suggest certain ideas to men when they're displayed in the right way.

We said hello and I introduced myself. He could hardly look up, and then mainly at my chest, without taking his eyes off my legs. All is well thus far.

It's time for me to take on my duty. I stood up, moved to the edge of the bed, and bent down as though I was going to examine him. I scrutinized my enhanced cleavage closely. "How are we doing today?" I inquired in my most polished tone. It seems like nurses say "we" all the time.

His eyes remained focused on my breasts as he responded, "Oh, the usual," with a meek smile. His eyes were downcast as he said, "But I have to confess something to you. I've been very bad; I haven't followed the doctor's orders or taken my meds. I hope you don't have to punish me."

Smite him? Surgeon? I see. Even though I'm not the sharpest pencil in the drawer, no one has ever called me stupid. That's how it was supposed to be, then?

"Oh yes," I responded. I decided to let him take the lead

here. "If you've been a bad boy, you'll have to be punished. Doctor's orders, you know. What shall it be?"

He grinned knowingly and continued, "The last nurse spanked me."

"Very well, then. I shall have to do the same. You know, though, spanking is hard work. I'll have to take off my blouse, if you don't mind."

With great grace, he consented and gazed hungrily as I carefully undid my blouse and took it off.

I started to get into this. "Now you roll over on your stomach like a good boy." I pulled down the sheet to reveal his ass once he was finished. Of course he was nude.

I gave him a few hand slaps on the behind.

That didn't really hurt, he said. "You'll have to do better."

Fine with me. I hit him with a couple of strong, hard blows.

I pondered his wife's thoughts on the disturbance.

"Much better," he remarked. "I promise I'll be good."

"I hope so. Oh, look. Now you've gone and gotten me all sweaty. Here," I replied, "just feel the sweat on my breasts."

He half turned, and I held his hand over the spot where my breasts protruded past the bra. I assisted him in rolling over to the other side. From the corner of my eye, I could see that his erection was getting bigger.

I said, "Still too hot." "You really made me work hard. The least you can do now is to take my bra off and lick some of the sweat off my breasts."

He obeyed without hesitation. He immediately released them and caressed my breasts, rubbing his hands over them, squeezing and massaging them in a pleasurable manner, and spending time on my nipples. It was starting to get quite enjoyable! I do enjoy what I do.

Leaning down, I let him to savor my right breast. His cock stiffened, and I saw it out of the corner of my eye. My nipples were also reacting well.

"Oh my," I exclaimed, staring him in the face. "You have tumescence." I'm not sure whether he understood the term, but it sounded clinical to me. "Well, that's something we can treat. Just lie back, and I'll take care of it. There's no need to worry about the doctor."

Sometimes I feel like I should have majored in drama instead of English. "First, though, I'll have to examine it more closely before I can make a full diagnosis." Was I excellent at this stuff or what?

I heard him take a breath and felt his member gently as I reached down to kiss it a few times, letting my breasts lightly brush over his abdomen and gently probing the slit with my tongue. I could taste his pre-cum. I slid my mouth down over him until I had a couple of inches of cock inside my mouth, and then my lips, lubricated by his pre-cum, slid easily over the bulbous tip and firmly embraced his shaft. It felt good, and I could feel his cock pulsating on my tongue and becoming more rigid.

I get a heady sense of accomplishment (and, if I'm being honest with myself, a frisson of raw power) when I bring a man to a shuddering climax with my mouth. Truth be told, I was getting pretty hot thinking about it. But then my professional ethos kicked in, and, remembering how much this guy was paying me, I felt I needed to prolong this a bit more. Besides, the intensity of the ultimate release is always enhanced by a well-crafted buildup.

I gave his cock a couple of light sucks before grudgingly pulling off.

"Well, it appears that you are not responding to treatment,"

I murmured, sounding a little more hushed than I had meant to. We will need to use a little more aggression."

I got up and feigned that my skirt was giving me difficulties.

I said, "Damn, it's stuck again." I noticed that all pretense of his "sickness" had disappeared when he sat up, and I knew that he was all mine going forward.

He fumbled with my skirt, finally succeeding in unsnapping it so that it slid to the floor, and I climbed out of it and onto the bed, gently nudging him back onto the pillows and straddling him, knowing that sexy guys find them attractive (they make me feel attractive too), and feeling his hard cock throbbing against my pussy through the thin nylon of my panties, he let go of my breasts long enough for him to run his hands over my waist, then back up my thighs, and over my stockings

I positioned my pelvis above him, bracing myself on his chest and directing his hand to my crotch.

"These panties always get in the way of this cure," I replied. "Here, just hold the middle part off to one side for a moment."

He did, and I was thrilled to feel his fingers on my sensitive labia. As he moved, the back of his hand lightly touched my clit, and I gasped uncontrollably. I wanted that big stiff cock inside me, and I wanted it now! I reached between my legs and grabbed it, lifted it, and positioned its head at the opening of my vagina, then lowered myself onto him. We both sighed as he slid into me, and my goodness, it felt wonderful in there. He pushed up as I descended, and I spread my legs as much as I could to allow him to get really deep into me.

My mouth was open, trying to keep up with my breathing, and my eyes were closed, so my mouth was closed. All thoughts of role-playing went out the window, and I had only one goal, now, to feel that wonderful fire course through me. Only a tiny iota of professionalism remained, struggling to remind me that my primary job was to pleasure the client. I had to hold my own gratification off until after I finished moaning.

I could feel my vagina contracting, milking him, pressing my pelvis hard into his, trying for the last millimeter of penetration. I knew I was squirting all over him, my own fluids mingling with his copious discharge, flooding me and him at the same time. His powerful life-giving cock grew and stiffened inside me, stretching the walls of my vagina. I could feel his orgasm gathering. His abdomen contracted. He gave a deep and heartfelt groan and then abruptly released inside me, deep in.

We stayed intertwined for many seconds after we had both done. Our breathing slowed, my thoughts reluctantly returned from wherever it had gone, and I grinned down at him, feeling him deflate inside of me.

I got up and rolled off him, his cock sliding out of my pussy and wilting to one side. I got back up and wiped him off, using a towel that someone had helpfully left beside the bed. Then I got up and used the towel to capture the last of his dripping semen.

Still a little breathless, I added, "I'm happy to say that I think the cure for your tumescence worked. I think that I can give the doctor a very good report."

He said, "You're right. I feel much better now. Tell the doctor that I'm delighted with his new nurse, please."

"Thank you," I said, and with that, I changed back into my clothes. Just enough of my professionalism was left to remind me to take my time, caress each piece of feminine apparel sensuously and slowly, showing a reluctance to hide the nice parts. Guys love a good reverse strip tease, almost as much as the actual taking off part. My underwear was still a little damp, but I'd have to put up with that for the time being. Oh, the things that women must endure!

I guess I reddened, but I gave Gregg one final, lingering smile and walked out, leaving his wife waiting outside. I had forgotten about her in all the before.

"Please, don't feel embarrassed," she said. From what I've heard, it seems that you performed an excellent and proficient job. I'm pleased for my spouse. I'm grateful. Would you kindly take a seat for a short while? Do you need anything from me?

"No, thank you. I'm fine." Well, except that there was some sperm on my underwear. What the hell, though?

After turning, she entered the bedroom. In a brief moment, she returned outside.

"Gregg is indeed very happy. He asked me to give you this. Please consider it as coming from both of us."

"This" ended up being an additional hundred. It's nice to be valued. Still, having the wife congratulate me for fucking her husband had to be the weirdest compliment I've ever received. Still, her comments had an impact. Even though she was still in need of my sympathy, she was able to convince me that I had provided her with expert assistance.

She remarked, "I hope we'll see you again, soon."

I said something and gave a noncommittal smile. I'd be damned, but I wasn't going to do this on a daily basis; I knew James would be upset with me and probably not understand. For my taste, just too weird and unpleasant. In addition, the variety of my work is one of its best aspects. Hell, I might as well get married if I wanted to fuck the same guy every single week! Besides, I wouldn't want to become stale, would I? It's not nearly as much fun for either of us, and guys can tell when you're just phoning it in.

I didn't mind at all that my underwear was wet because I was feeling quite good about myself on the drive home.

Acknowledgments

The Glory of this book's success goes to God Almighty and my beautiful Family, Fans, Readers & well-wishers, Customers, and Friends for their endless support and encouragement.

About The Author

I've spent nearly a decade penning romantic novels. As a passionate writer of erotica, I craft dark, romantic erotica. Anime Naked Truth Se of Sacred Sexuality: Forbidden Seducing Short Stories of an Erotica Nude Sexy Girl Poster. Alongside Erotic Mystery Fiction, Victorian Erotica Sex, Black & African American Erotica, Euthanasia, Daddy Teaching, Forced Domination, Alpha Monster Cuckold, and BDSM for Adults, there's an Erotic Fiction in Kinky Family. I write dark, sensual romance because I adore the power of darkness and everything that it entails. Romance novels have always been my favorite kind of books, and now I'm writing them. The idea that you will like reading and enjoying my fiction as much as I enjoy pushing the frontiers of sexual pleasure in my writing thrills me more than anything else.